Written &
illustrated by
Shoo Rayner

WALKER BOOKS
AND SUBSIDIARIES
LONDON · BOSTON · SYDNEY · AUCKLAND

Chapter One

When Betty Pointer was a baby, she hardly ever made a sound. Most babies gurgle and cry; Betty made signs.
A thumbs up meant everything was OK.

Pointing to her tummy meant
she was hungry.

And holding her nose meant
she had a stinky nappy, so would
someone please change it!

One day, before Betty could talk, her mother gave her something new to eat. "It's alphabet spaghetti," she said.

Betty's eyes lit up. She began pushing
the letters around her plate.
"Don't play with your food, dear," said
her mother.

But Betty carried on sorting the spaghetti letters, licking her fingers from time to time.

"Betty," said her mum, "I told you not to play with your food!"
Then she looked at Betty's plate and got a big surprise.

Betty's dad swung her up in the air.
"You're a genius, Alpha Betty!" he
laughed. And that was how Betty got
her nickname.

Chapter Two

Was Betty a genius? Maybe – maybe not. But she certainly loved signs. When she got a bit older, she made them with toy bricks.

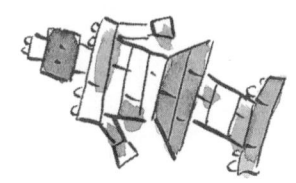

doll

food

this way

that way

ice cream

chocolate

Then she learned to read them.
This was very useful when she needed
to go to the toilet,

Toilet ▶

or when she wanted to know if the
library was open.

Library
Opening Times
Mon . 9 5
Tue ... 9 5
Wed ... 3 5
Thur... 9 1
Fri 9 5
Sat ... 9 12

Betty read everything: packets and tins, street names, shop signs and posters.

She even read the postcards in the
newsagent's window.

Help Wanted
Three old ladies
locked in lavatory.
Please come round between
Monday and Saturday.

And when anyone asked Betty what she wanted to be when she grew up, she smiled and said, "I want to be a sign-maker, of course!"

Chapter Three

Betty made signs whenever she could.
She made them on fridges and on
Scrabble boards.

She made them with
squirty cream,

Yummy!

baked beans

repeat after me

and mashed potato.

SMASHING

She made them for special events.

And for Christmases and birthdays she always asked for paints and brushes so that she could make MORE signs!

Chapter Four

When Betty Pointer left school, she opened a sign-making shop. It wasn't very big, but Betty was very proud of it. Lots of people came to buy her signs.

But one day a huge factory opened on the edge of town. Tacky Tim's Sign Superstore delivered signs to your door and even had a drive-in, while-u-wait sign-making department.

Tacky Tim made plastic signs on machines run by computers.

He could make three hundred sticky-backed signs before Betty could open a pot of paint.

Stick 'em up!

TACKY TIM'S STICKY BACKED PLASTIC

The new signs were bright and cheap
and you could stick them anywhere.
Everyone went mad!

The whole town was covered in cheap, plastic signs. Betty sighed every time she saw Tacky Tim's delivery vans. "More stupid signs," she said to herself.

Soon Betty had no customers at all.

Chapter Five

But as the weeks went by, Tacky Tim's signs began to look a bit tired.
The sticky backs lost their stick and peeled off.

Some of the letters faded ...

...and bits started to fall off.

People were fed up with Tacky Tim and
his signs.

Chapter Six

In the meantime Betty had thought of new and exciting ways to make signs that weren't sticky or plastic.

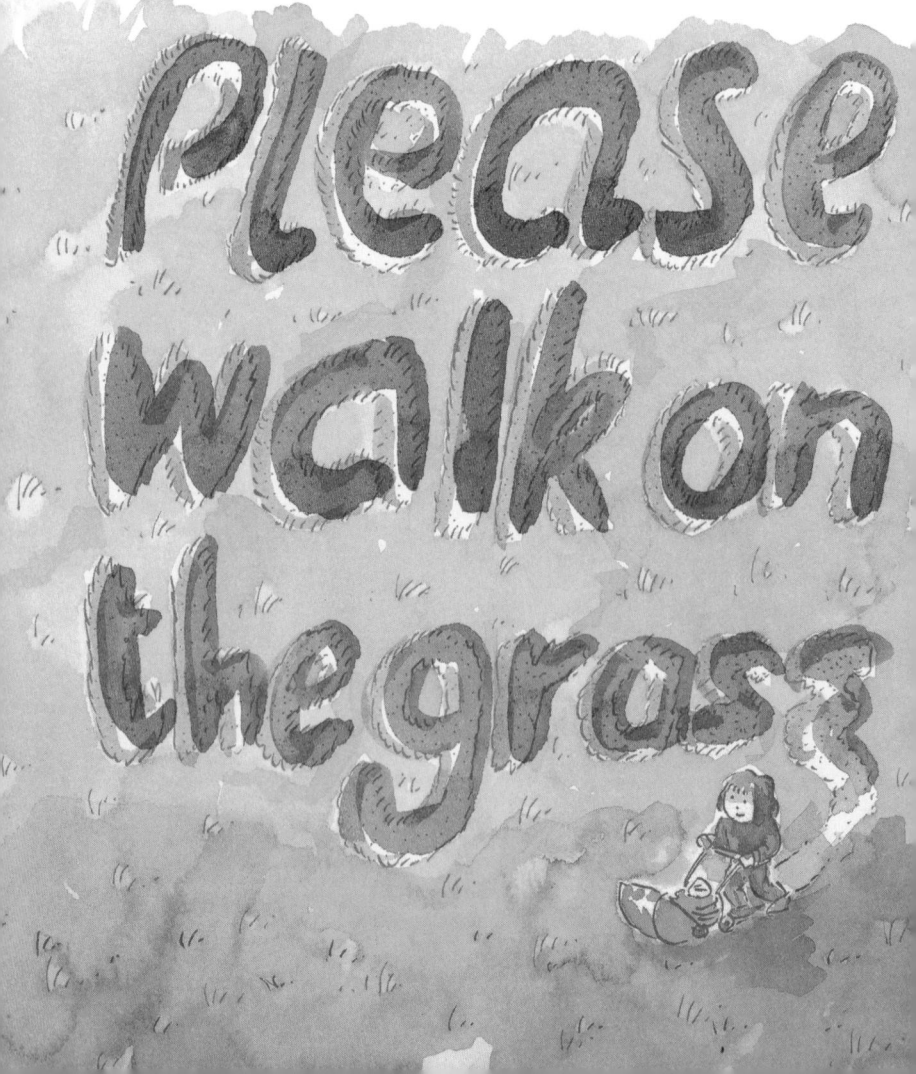

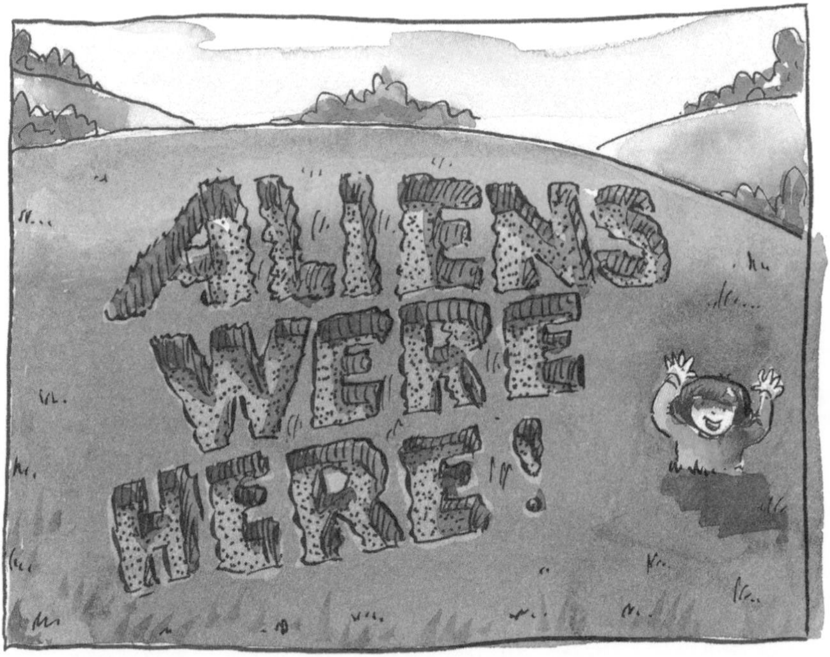
ALIENS WERE HERE!

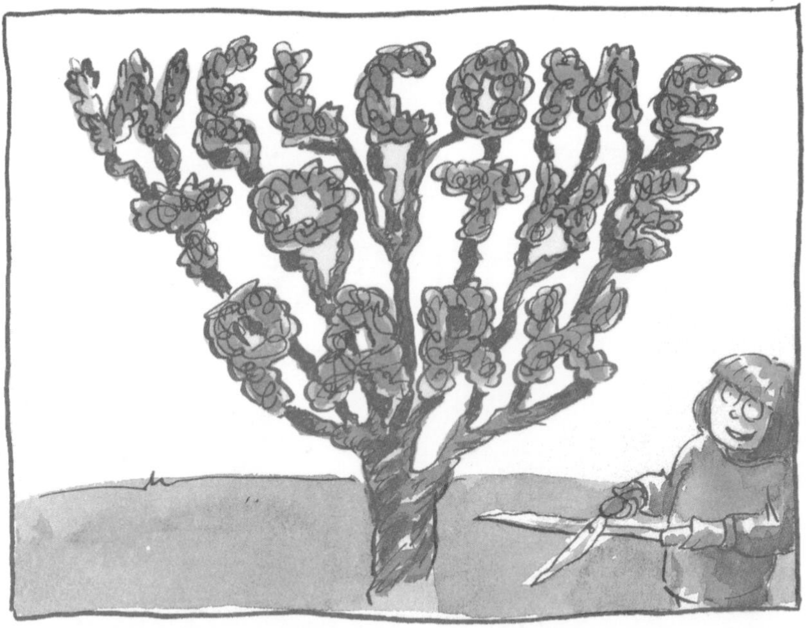
WELCOME

Betty's signs made people smile.

HUG A
TREE
Make it
BARK!

Soon they were queuing up outside her shop again.

Tacky Tim was desperate.

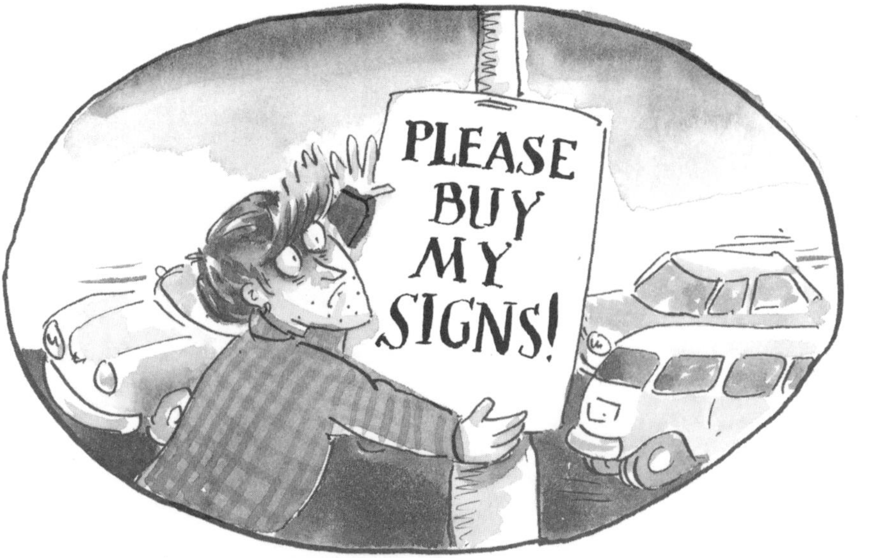
PLEASE BUY MY SIGNS!

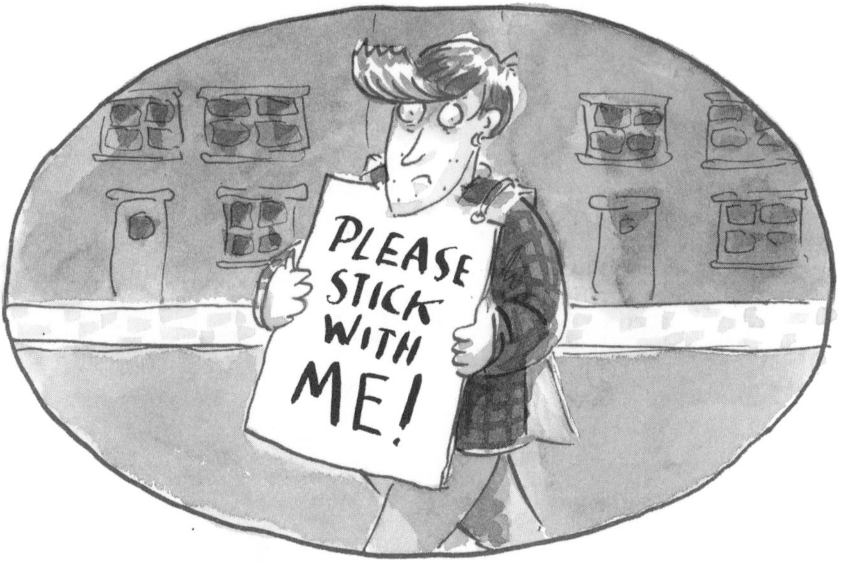
PLEASE STICK WITH ME!

He stuck signs all over the town.
But it was no good. Nobody wanted
Tacky Tim's tacky signs any more.

HAT WAY
ED & BREAK ST
RUBBISH
OV
ACKY INS
PIG SALE
AP
WASTE.CO.
FOR
TRASH
What a load of rubbish!

One day Betty was asked to make a special new sign. "I'd be happy to!" she said.

She sawed the wood and painted it
carefully with her best brush. It said …

For Julie Vockins

First published 2006 by Walker Books Ltd
87 Vauxhall Walk, London SE11 5HJ

2 4 6 8 10 9 7 5 3 1

© 2006 Shoo Rayner

The right of Shoo Rayner to be identified
as author and illustrator of this work has been
asserted by him in accordance with the Copyright,
Designs and Patents Act 1988

This book has been typeset in ITC Officina Sans

Handlettering by Shoo Rayner

Printed in China

British Library Cataloguing in Publication Data:
a catalogue record for this book
is available from the British Library

ISBN-13: 978-1-84428-124-4
ISBN-10: 1-84428-124-8

www.walkerbooks.co.uk